Tim and the Blanket Thief

Copyright © 1993 by John Prater

All rights reserved. No part of this book may be reproduced or
transmitted in any form or by any means, electronic or
mechanical, including photocopying, recording, or by any
information storage and retrieval system, without permission in
writing from the Publisher.

Atheneum
Macmillan Publishing Company
866 Third Avenue
New York, NY 10022

Macmillan Publishing Company is part of the Maxwell Communication
Group of Companies.

First Atheneum edition

Published originally in Great Britain by The Bodley Head

Printed in Hong Kong by Wing King Tong Printing Company (1993) Ltd.

Library of Congress Catalog Card Number 93–6563
ISBN 0–689–31881–2

TIM
AND THE
BLANKET THIEF

John Prater

ATHENEUM 1993 NEW YORK

Tim was a shy boy.
He wasn't very brave.

He didn't like noisy, messy fun or
being splashed or roughhousing.

He didn't like big adventures.

He only wanted to be alone and quiet,
with his special soft and sleepy blanket.
He took his blanket everywhere,
and kept it close by him always.

The other children would sometimes tease him by singing the "Blanket Thief Song"!

Look out! Beware the blanket thief
Who creeps around at night,
And steals away your favorite things
If you don't hug them tight!
They say he can be frightened off
If you put up a fight!
But none of us would ever dare
Face such an awful sight.

One dark and windy night Tim lay in bed, holding his blanket tight.
But when he fell asleep, he tossed and turned — and let it go!

A chilling blast of air blew through the bedroom, and Tim awoke to find his blanket gone.

He let out a little cry, which grew bigger, and bigger, and bigger...

until he yelled at the top of his voice,
"Come back, you thief! Give
me back my blanket!"

Tim leaped out into the night to catch the thief.

The streets were dark and empty.

The woods were darker still.

The path was steep, the mud was deep, and although his heart beat fast, Tim never took his eyes off the wicked rogue ahead.

The weather grew wild, and the waves crashed loud.

But Tim bravely kept going on. He knew that he was getting close to
the blanket thief's dreadful lair.

He took a deep breath, then boldly entered the dim and rocky cave.

The startled blanket thief
grew bigger, and bigger,
and bigger, let out a
horrid scream, and
turned to pounce
on Tim....

But Tim did not run. He stood quite still and faced that awful sight.
"Give me back my blanket!" he yelled, snatching it from the thief's grasp.
The blanket thief's horrid scream grew fainter, until it was no more than
the distant whistling of the wind. His huge darkness grew pale and thin,
until it was no more than the smoke curling from the fire.

"Phew!" said Tim. "Serves you right." He knew there was nothing left of the villain. The blanket thief was gone forever.

Tim gathered together all the blankets, teddy bears, and best-loved toys in the wicked robber's hoard.

The boat was full for the journey home.

Everyone cheered Tim the hero for being the bravest boy ever.

But even the bravest boy ever still cuddled
his blanket for just a little longer.